La Mariposa

Francisco Jiménez

Illustrated by Simón Silva

HOUGHTON MIFFLIN COMPANY
BOSTON 1998

Text copyright © 1998 by Francisco Jiménez
Illustrations copyright © 1998 by Simón Silva
All rights reserved. For information about permission to reproduce
selections from this book, write to Permissions, Houghton Mifflin Company,
215 Park Avenue South, New York, New York 10003.
The type of this book is set in 15/20 pt. New Baskerville Semi Bold.
The illustrations are gouache on Crescent Cold Press illustration board.
Book design by Carol Goldenberg

Library of Congress Cataloging-in-Publication Data
Jiménez, Francisco.
La mariposa / by Francisco Jiménez; illustrated by Simón Silva.
p. cm.
Summary: Because he can only speak Spanish, Francisco, son of a migrant
worker, has trouble when he begins first grade, but his fascination with the
caterpillar in the classroom helps him begin to fit in.
ENG ISBN 0-395-81663-7   SP ISBN 0-395-91738-7
[I. Schools—Fiction. 2. Mexican Americans—Fiction.]
I. Silva, Simón, ill. II. Title.
PZ7.J57525Lam 1998
[E]—dc20   96-27664
CIP   AC

Manufactured in the United States of America
HOR 10 9 8 7 6 5 4 3 2 1

To my teachers, whose faith in my ability and guidance
helped me break the migrant circuit.
—F. J.

To the people I will always remember, my teachers:
your words and inspiration will continue to
make a difference.
¡Si Se Puede!
—S. S.

Early Monday morning, Francisco got up to get ready. Quickly he pulled on his overalls, which he hated because he thought the suspenders made him look foolish. But he found the soft, bright flannel shirt Mamá had just bought at the Goodwill store. Then he put on his favorite cap.

"Quítatela en la clase," his older brother, Roberto, warned him, for he had been to school before and knew it was bad manners to wear a hat in class.

"Gracias," Francisco told him, taking it off. But after his breakfast and just before heading out, he decided to wear the cap. Papá always wore one, and how could Francisco feel dressed for first grade without it? He would remember to take it off in class.

"*Adiós,* Mamá," Francisco and Roberto called as they headed out to catch the school bus.

"*Adiós, hijos,*" she answered, "*Que Dios los bendiga.*" Papá had already left to thin lettuce, the only work he could find in late January. Mamá stayed home to take care of little José and to set up their new home in Tent City.

When the school bus arrived, Francisco took the window seat next to his brother so that he could watch the rows of lettuce and cauliflower go whizzing by. He thought the furrows looked like giant legs running alongside. The bus kept stopping to pick up kids, and with each stop, the noise inside grew louder. Some kids were yelling at the top of their lungs. Francisco did not know what they were saying because he could speak only Spanish, and they were all speaking English. He was getting a headache. Roberto had his eyes closed and was frowning. Francisco did not disturb him. He figured his brother was getting a headache, too.

When they got to school, Roberto walked Francisco to the principal's office. Mr. Sims, the principal, was a tall red-headed man who listened patiently to Roberto. "My little brother," Roberto said, using the little English he knew, "is *en primer grado*."

Mr. Sims walked Francisco to the first grade classroom, and as soon as he saw the bright electric lights, shiny wood floor, and the warm heater in the corner, Francisco liked the room. It was not at all like his family's green army tent, with its hard dirt floor.

Mr. Sims introduced Francisco to his teacher, Miss Scalapino, who smiled and repeated his name, "Francisco." It was the only word Francisco understood the whole time she and the principal talked. They repeated it each time they glanced at him. After Mr. Sims left, she showed Francisco to his desk at the end of the row of desks closest to the windows. There were no other kids in the room.

Francisco sat at his desk and ran his hand over its wooden top. It was full of scratches and dark ink spots. He lifted the top and inside were a box of crayons, a yellow ruler, and a thick pencil. Looking around the room, he saw under the window, right next to his desk, a caterpillar in a large jar. It was yellowish green with black bands, and it moved very slowly, without making any sound.

Just as Francisco was about to reach into the jar to gently touch the caterpillar, the bell rang. Kids lined up outside the classroom doorway and then walked in quietly and took their seats. Some of them looked at Francisco and giggled. They made him nervous. He turned his head away from them and looked at the caterpillar in the jar. He did this every time someone looked at him.

Miss Scalapino started speaking to the class and Francisco did not understand a word she said. The more she spoke, the more Francisco wanted to be at home. He tried to pay attention because he wanted to understand. But by the end of the day he got very tired of hearing Miss Scalapino talk because the sounds still made no sense to him. He got a bad headache, and that night, when he went to bed, he heard her voice in his head.

For days Francisco tried to listen, but he always went home with a bad headache, until he learned a way out. When his head began to hurt from trying to understand, he let his mind wander. Sometimes he imagined himself flying out of the classroom and over the fields where Papá worked.

"*¡Hola, Papá!*" he would say, landing next to him.
But Francisco was careful to not let the teacher
catch him thinking about flying. He would look at
the teacher and pretend he was listening. Papá had
told him it was disrespectful not to pay attention,
especially to grownups.

When the teacher spoke the children's names, though, Francisco would listen. He liked their sound. "Molly" sounded like *"mole"* in Spanish and "Pat" sounded like *"pato."* The one he learned first was "Curtis" because Curtis was the biggest and most popular kid in the class. He was always chosen captain when the kids formed teams. Francisco was the smallest kid in the class, and he did not know English, so he was chosen last.

Francisco liked Arthur better. Arthur was one of the boys who knew a little Spanish. During recess, they would play on the swings, and Francisco would pretend to be a Mexican movie star, like Jorge Negrete or Pedro Infante, riding a horse and singing the *corridos* he heard on the car radio. He taught the songs to Arthur as they swung back and forth, going as high as they could.

But if Miss Scalapino heard them speaking Spanish, she would say "NO!" with her whole body. Her head turned left and right a hundred times a second and her index finger moved from side to side as fast as a windshield wiper. "English! English!" she repeated. Arthur avoided Francisco whenever she was around.

Often during recess, Francisco stayed with the caterpillar. Sometimes it was hard to spot him because he blended in with the green leaves and twigs. Every day, Francisco brought him leaves from the pepper trees that grew on the playground.

Just in front of the caterpillar, lying on top of the cabinet, was a picture book of caterpillars and butterflies. Francisco liked to look through it page by page, studying all the pictures and running his fingers lightly over the caterpillars and the bright wings of the butterflies and the many patterns on them. He knew caterpillars turned into butterflies because Roberto had told him. But just how did they do it? How long did it take? The words written underneath each picture in big black letters could tell him, he knew. So he tried to figure them out by looking at the pictures. He did this so many times he could close his eyes and see the words. But he still could not understand what they meant.

By the time Papá started topping carrots in March, art had become Francisco's favorite time at school. He did not understand Miss Scalapino when she explained the art lessons, so she let him do whatever he wanted. He drew all kinds of animals, but mostly birds and butterflies. He sketched them in pencil and then colored them, using every color in his crayon box. He got pretty good at drawing butterflies. Miss Scalapino even tacked one of his pictures up on the board for everyone to see. After a couple of weeks it disappeared, and he did not know how to ask where it had gone.

One cold Thursday morning, during recess, Francisco was the only kid on the playground without a jacket. The principal must have noticed that he was shivering because, after school, he took him to his office and pulled out a green jacket from a large cardboard box full of used clothes. He handed it to Francisco and gestured for him to try it on. It smelled like graham crackers. Francisco put it on, but it was too big, so he rolled up the sleeves about two inches. Then he took it home and showed it off to his parents. He liked it because it was green and it hid his suspenders.

The next day Francisco wore his new jacket to school. He was on the playground waiting for the first bell to ring when he saw Curtis coming at him like an angry bull. Curtis aimed his head at Francisco, pulled his arms straight back with his hands clenched, and ran up to him, yelling. Francisco did not understand him, but he knew it had something to do with the jacket because Curtis began to pull on it, trying to take it off. Next thing Francisco knew, he and Curtis were on the ground, wrestling. Kids circled around them. He could hear them yelling Curtis's name and something else. Francisco knew he had no chance; Curtis was so much bigger and stronger. But he held on tight to his jacket. Why should he let him take it? Curtis pulled on one of the sleeves so hard that it ripped at the shoulder. He pulled on the right pocket and it ripped, too.

Then Miss Scalapino's face appeared above them. She pushed Curtis off of Francisco, grabbed Francisco by the back of his collar, and picked him up off the ground! It took all the power he had not to cry.

Later Arthur told Francisco in Spanish that Curtis said the jacket was his, that he had lost it at the beginning of the year. He also told Francisco that the teacher said Curtis and he were being punished. They had to sit on the bench during all the recesses that week.

For the rest of the day, Francisco could not even pretend he was paying attention. He laid his head on top of his desk and closed his eyes. He couldn't even imagine himself flying over the fields to Papá anymore. The teacher called his name, but Francisco did not answer. He heard her walk up to him.

She gently shook him by the shoulders. Again, he did not answer. Miss Scalapino must have thought he was dead asleep because she left him alone, even when it was time for recess and everyone left the room.

Once the room was quiet, Francisco slowly opened his eyes. He had had them closed for so long that the sunlight coming through the windows was too bright. He rubbed his eyes with the back of his hands and then looked for the caterpillar in the jar. Where was it? Was it hidden? He put his hand in the jar and lightly stirred the leaves. Then he saw it. The caterpillar had spun itself into a cocoon! It had attached itself to a small twig, and now it looked like a tiny, cotton bulb. Gently, Francisco stroked it with his index finger. It seemed so peaceful.

At the end of the school day, Miss Scalapino gave Francisco a note to take home to his parents. Papá and Mamá did not know how to read, but as soon as they saw his swollen upper lip and the scratches on his cheek, they knew what the note said. When he told them what had happened, they both frowned and glared at him. Papá finally said, "But it's good you didn't disrespect the teacher."

Francisco never saw the green jacket again. It had gone back to Curtis, who didn't wear it any more because the days were growing warmer. Francisco never spoke to Curtis, but slowly he began to say a few English words, like "thank you" and "okay" to Arthur and the other kids and sometimes to his teacher.

On Wednesday, May 23, a few days before the end of the school year, Miss Scalapino told everyone to sit down. Then Francisco did not understand any more of what she said, until he heard her say "Francisco" as she held up a blue ribbon. From her desk, she picked up his drawing of the butterfly that had disappeared from the board so many weeks before. Holding it up high for everyone to see, she walked up to Francisco and handed him the drawing and the blue silk ribbon that had a number 1 printed on it in gold. *¡Qué sorpresa!* He had received first prize for his drawing! He was so proud he wanted to run home right away to tell Papá and Mamá. All the other kids, including Curtis, rushed over to see his ribbon.

That afternoon, during free period, Francisco went over to check on the caterpillar. He turned the jar around trying to see the cocoon. Then he gasped. It was beginning to crack open! "Look, look," he cried out, pointing to it. The whole class, like a swarm of bees, rushed over to the counter. Miss Scalapino took the jar and placed it on top of a desk in the middle of the classroom so everyone could see it. For a while they all stood there, watching the butterfly come out of its cocoon in slow motion, like magic.

At the end of the day, just before the last bell, Miss Scalapino picked up the jar and took the class outside to the playground. She placed the jar on the ground and everyone circled around.

Francisco had a hard time seeing over the other kids, so Miss Scalapino called him and motioned for him to open the jar. Breaking through the circle, he knelt on the ground and unscrewed the top. Swiftly, the butterfly flew into the air, fluttering its orange and black wings up and down.

"*¡Qué hermosa!*" Francisco said—but softly, under his breath, so no one would hear him speak Spanish.

Miss Scalapino must have heard, though. "*¡Qué hermosa!*" she repeated, smiling down at Francisco. "How beautiful!"

After school, Francisco waited in line for his bus in front of the playground. In his right hand he carried the blue ribbon, and in his left, the drawing. Arthur and Curtis came up and stood behind him to wait for their bus. Curtis motioned for Francisco to show him the drawing again. He held it up so Curtis could see it.

"He really likes it, Francisco," Arthur said to him in Spanish.

"How do you say *'es tuyo' en inglés?*" he asked Arthur.

"It's yours," Arthur answered.

"It's yours," Francisco repeated and handed the drawing to Curtis.

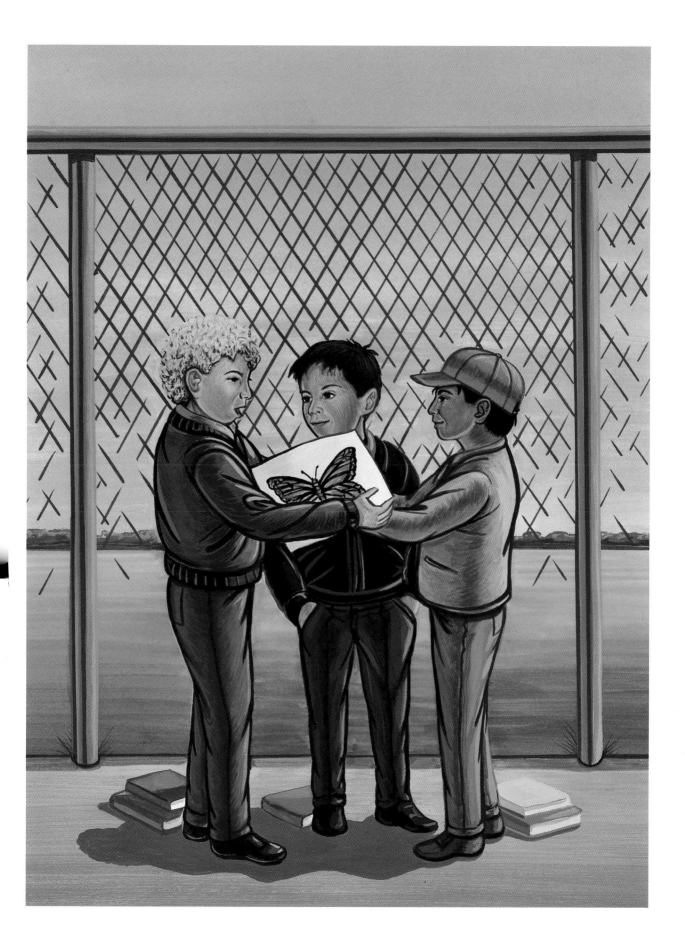

Glossary

Adiós, hijos (a-dee-OS EE-hos): Goodbye, sons.

Corridos (cor-REE-dos): Mexican folkloric songs or ballads

En inglés (en in-GLAYS): In English

En primer grado (en pree-MERR GRAH-doe): In first grade

Es tuyo (es TOO-yo): It's yours.

Gracias (GRAH-see-ahs): Thank you.

¡Hola! (OH-lah): Hello! or Hi!

La mariposa (lah mah-ree-PO-sah): Butterfly

Mamá (mah-MAH): Mama

Mole (MO-lay): Black or green chili sauce

Papá (pah-PAH): Papa

pato (PAH-to): Duck

Que Dios los bendiga (kay dee-OS los ben-DEE-gah): May God bless you.

¡Qué hermosa! (kay er-MO-sah): How beautiful!

¡Qué sorpresa! (kay sor-PRAY-sah): What a surprise!

Quítatela en la clase (KEE-ta-tay-lah en lah KLAH-say): Take it (the cap) off in class.